THE WICKED SLAPSHOT

by Irene Punt

illustrations by
Bojan Redzic

Scholastic Canada Ltd.
Toronto New York London Auckland Sydney
Mexico City New Delhi Hong Kong Buenos Aires

Scholastic Canada Ltd.
604 King Street West, Toronto, Ontario M5V 1E1, Canada

Scholastic Inc.
557 Broadway, New York, NY 10012, USA

Scholastic Australia Pty Limited
PO Box 579, Gosford, NSW 2250, Australia

Scholastic New Zealand Limited
Private Bag 94407, Botany, Manukau 2163, New Zealand

Scholastic Children's Books
Euston House, 24 Eversholt Street,
London NW1 1DB, UK

www.scholastic.ca

Library and Archives Canada Cataloguing in Publication
Punt, Irene, 1955-
The wicked slapshot / Irene Punt.
ISBN 0-439-94897-5
I. Title.
PS8581.U56W52 2006   jC813'.54   C2006-900822-1

ISBN-10 0-439-94897-5 / ISBN-13 978-0-439-94897-5

11 10 9   Printed in Canada 121   14 15 16

MIX
Paper from
responsible sources
FSC
www.fsc.org   FSC® C004071

Contents

To my boys — Harty, Tom and Dave;
my parents; and my pals — Anne, Joanne
and Vivien. Thanks, team!

— I.P.

Hockey Camp

It was the hottest day of August and the first
day of Champs Hockey Camp. Tom crouched
on the driveway, checking his hockey bag.

"Skates, helmet, jersey, shin pads, shoulder pads, elbow pads, pants." He glanced down the street and then burrowed to the bottom of the bag — where dried-up sports socks and used-up tape rolls lurk. He continued, "Neck guard, mouthguard, gloves, hockey socks, sock tape, jock. Okay. Everything's here." He zipped up the bag.

The street was still empty. His friends were nowhere in sight. He picked up his lucky stick and shot a couple of tape rolls onto the lawn.

"Hurry up," said his mom, rushing toward the car. "Get your stuff in the trunk."

Tom strained to lift his bag. It felt as if it were filled with boulders. "Ugh." He dropped it down again and plunked himself on top. "It's not fair!"

"What's the matter?" asked Mom, confused. "You've been counting the days till hockey camp all summer."

Tom sighed. "Mark's on a trip with his family. Jordan's gone to goalie camp. And now Stuart's wrecked his ankle skateboarding. I wanted to go to hockey camp with my friends. It won't be any fun without them."

"You don't need a friend at camp," said Mom. "Hockey's your friend." She gave him a pat on the back. "You'll have lots of fun. C'mon, it's *hockey!*"

Tom looked up and forced a smile as he heaved his bag into the trunk. He knew the ride to the arena was going to be lonely and boring without his friends. Together they were a team. They all loved hockey — all year round.

Mom backed out of the driveway. Tom reached over and found his favourite station on the radio. His mom turned up the volume two notches. And everything seemed a little better.

At the Arena

Bright sunlight lit up the silver letters: Centennial Arena.

Tom carried his stick over his shoulder and lugged his hockey bag through the sliding doors. Lots of information was printed on the message board in thick, black letters. Tom headed over to read it.

Everyone laughed when they read the message. Even Tom. He walked past the snack counter, through some doors, behind the spectator stands, down a long hall and into dressing room #6. He propped up his stick against the others in the corner.

Tom scanned the room. It was crowded

and noisy and everyone seemed to know somebody. Some of the boys were wearing the same team T–shirts with Hawaiian shorts. They jostled and joked loudly, like best friends. *Where should I sit?* Tom began to worry. *Relax*, he told himself. But it was weird not recognizing one face. It was weird not having Stuart, Mark and Jordan with him.

5

He let out his breath and sat down on the bench next to a boy with red hair.

"Hi," said Tom.

"Hi," said the boy, concentrating on taping his socks.

Tom started rooting through his bag, looking for his jock. He suited up quickly. By the time he was tightening his skates, everyone else was dressed and ready to go. Now the change room looked familiar. *Hockey play-*

ers are hockey players, thought Tom, seeing everyone tall in their skates and anxious for ice. Just before he put on his helmet, he wrote his name on a piece of masking tape and stuck it on the front, above the face mask. He could feel the excitement, the nearness of hockey, as they filed out of the room. He couldn't wait to play.

Tom followed the rubber flooring to the entrance gate where the players lined up, waiting. The Zamboni made one last sweep down the middle of the ice and headed for the parking stall. The driver jumped down and closed the wide doors.

"We can go on now!" shouted one of the kids.

Fourteen boys and four girls launched themselves one by one onto the freshly flooded rink. Tom loved the feel of the smooth ice under his blades. He glided out and then bent down automatically to stretch his back.

BOOM! The heavy gate banged shut and was secured with a big metal latch.

Here we go, thought Tom, and a smile spread across his face.

Ninety-Nine Laps

A whistle blew. At centre ice a tall man with curly hair was waving them over.

"I'm Coach Dave. Welcome to the coolest place in town!" he announced, tipping his Calgary Flames cap.

Everyone laughed.

"Now for my icebreaker question," Coach Dave continued. "What was Wayne Gretzky's number?"

The red-haired boy called out, "99!" before Tom could answer.

Coach Dave had a sly look on his face. "Today is Power Skating day. In honour of The

Great One, let's skate 99 laps around the rink."

"99 laps!" gasped the kids.

Tom felt as if he had swallowed a puck. He could never skate 99 laps!

"Just kidding." Coach Dave winked. "We'll start with nine. Nine fast ones. In hockey we play one goal, one period and one game at a time."

Coach Dave blew his whistle and the players took off. Tom's blades cut into the ice, and he thought, *I can easily skate nine fast laps.*

Coach Dave shouted, "Heads up! Extend your leg!"

By the third lap, Tom forgot all about missing his friends.

Coach Dave shouted, "Bend your knees! Use your arms!"

By the fourth lap, Tom forgot all about summer.

Coach Dave shouted, "Pick up the pace!"

By the fifth lap, Tom noticed the red-haired boy again. The name tag on his helmet said *Harty*. They skated neck and neck at the front of the pack for five, six, seven laps.

"Keep going!" Harty shouted.

The last two laps were the hardest. Tom was out of breath and thirsty and his leg muscles burned. He looked at Harty. Harty's face was red and his strides were slowing down.

"Don't stop!" Tom shouted.

Finally, nine laps. Tom and Harty raised their arms and cheered. "We did it!" They coasted toward the water bottles lined up on the boards. Coach Dave flipped his stick around, and tapped the butt end twice. "Way to go!"

Tom and Harty, catching on to Coach Dave's signal, tapped their sticks, too. "Way to go!" Each picked up a water bottle and sucked back a big gulp.

Tom's heart was pounding. He tried to slow down his breathing. "Good work, Harty. You're fast."

"Yeah, good work . . . Tom." Harty smiled at him. "You're fast, too."

"Don't get too comfortable," warned Coach Dave, watching the last skater finish.

He rubbed his hands together. His eyes lit up. He cleared his throat and said, "At the whistle, nine laps — backwards!" He blew the whistle loud and strong.

"Let's go," said Harty, giving Tom a nudge with his elbow.

They circled the rink together.

Tom wondered how many laps they were going to skate in one day. *What if Coach Dave makes us skate nine laps eleven times? Nah*, he thought, *Coach Dave said he was joking about 99 laps. But was he?*

At the end of the day, Tom sat on the arena steps in the hot sun, waiting for his dad. His knees hurt and his stomach growled for dinner. He hadn't felt this great all summer.

Harty stumbled out the doors carrying his hockey bag. His head was soaked with sweat. "I sure feel like I skated 99 laps today. My legs are doing the wet noodle!"

Tom burst out laughing. "Mine, too!"

"Now we're The Great Ones!" laughed Harty, slapping a high five with Tom.

It isn't bad sitting out in the sun with a new friend, thought Tom. "Hey, where do you live, anyway?" he asked.

"Out near the airport. What about you?" Harty said.

"The other way. Near the reservoir." Tom shrugged.

"We couldn't live farther apart!" exclaimed Harty.

"No kidding." Tom knew it took at least 45 minutes to get from his house to the airport.

HONK! HONK! A truck blasted its horn.

Tom looked up. "Hey, that's my dad." He grabbed his stick and bag. "I'll see you tomorrow."

"Okay, see you tomorrow," waved Harty, spotting his mom.

Away they drove in opposite directions.

A Wicked Slapshot

On Tuesday, Tom retaped his stick before breakfast. He was in the car five minutes early. "Hurry up, Mom!" he called, tempted to honk the horn.

Mom rushed across the driveway and jumped in the car. "Hmm," she said. "Hockey fever again?"

"Yeah," he answered, smiling. He put on his sunglasses and punched in his favourite radio station. "It's Shooting Day. And I *looooooove* to shoot the puck!"

His mom agreed. "You *are* always practising your shot. Sometimes I think you practise in your sleep!" She laughed.

Tom nodded his head to the music. "I do!" He closed his eyes, visualizing his shot and the puck flying into the net.

— ● —

Coach Dave met the kids at centre ice with a large bucket of practice pucks. He showed them different ways to shoot the puck. Forehand. Backhand. Flip shot. Wrist shot. Snap shot. And a wicked slapshot.

"The best place to shoot is 'top shelf,' " he said. "That's at the top of the net. It's where Momma hides the cookies."

Everyone laughed.

"Okay, everybody grab a puck and spread out, facing the boards. Try at least . . ." Coach

Dave raised his voice, "99 shots!"

"You're on!" shouted Tom.

"I'm joking!" said Coach Dave. "Make it twenty."

Tom sighed. He would have loved to have 99 shots. He flipped a puck to Harty, then scooped one for himself.

BANG. BANG. Tom took slow, careful shots, then picked up speed. *BANG. BANG. BANG.*

The whistle blew. "Now, get a partner and

listen up," said Coach Dave. "The first pair to score a hat trick on the goalie wins pucks. Not just any pucks, but pucks autographed by me!"

Tom smiled at his new friend. "C'mon, Harty! You're my partner. We're the fastest skaters here!"

Harty winced. "You won't want me for a partner. I only got one goal last season. A hat trick is three."

"Don't worry. I read that Wayne Gretzky only got one goal in his first season of minor hockey," said Tom. He motioned to Harty, "Let's go! We can do it!"

"Okay," said Harty, sounding doubtful. He chewed on his mouth guard.

They got in line. Team after team charged down the ice, passing, passing, passing . . . *THWACK! THWACK!* The puck flew everywhere. It hit the spectator glass. It banged off the boards. It shot up into the stands.

And it was stopped by the goalie.

Finally it was Tom and Harty's turn. Coach Dave blew the whistle and they were off. Tom passed the puck right onto Harty's stick. Harty, striding powerfully up the outside, pulled the goalie over to the left while Tom raced up the middle. Just at the right

second, Harty passed the puck over to Tom, and Tom one-timed it into the net.

"Yeah, baby!" yelled Tom, punching his gloved fist in the air.

"Woo-ooo, Tom! You've got a wicked slap-shot!" shouted Harty.

"Thanks!" Tom grinned. He tapped Harty's shoulder. "*You* set me up perfectly!"

They stood in line, watching the puck as it slid and flew. *THWACK!* Two brothers scored. *THWACK!* Two girls scored. *THWACK!* Two big guys scored. Everyone hollered and cheered.

The goalie widened his stance. He positioned his stick. He braced himself.

"We can do it," Tom assured Harty. But on their second shift Harty's shot missed the net.

On their third try, Harty passed the puck to Tom and Tom scored again with another wicked slapshot.

"Wheeee . . . eew!" Harty whistled loudly.

"Hey, we're tied for the lead!" cried Tom. "Just one more goal and we win the . . . !" Before he could finish his sentence — *SWOOSH!* A puck flew into the net and the two-girl team leapt in the air, celebrating.

Tom's jaw dropped. "What?"

"Hat trick!" shouted Coach Dave. He flipped his stick around and tapped the butt end twice. Then he waved the winners over and presented them with the two autographed pucks. They held them up proudly, with big smiles on their faces.

Everyone else clapped and cheered, "YAAAAY!" But as Harty applauded he kept his head down and skated to the back.

———— ● ————

At the end of the day, Tom and Harty sat outside on the arena steps, sucking back slush drinks in the hot sun.

"These are better than rubber pucks any day!" said Tom, holding the cold cup to his cheek.

"I guess. But I still wish I got that goal." Harty looked at Tom. "Your slapshot is so wicked. How do you do it?"

Tom could see Harty's frustration and disappointment. "Practice, I guess. That's all. *Lots* of practice!"

HONK! HONK! The boys looked up. Their rides were waiting.

"See you tomorrow," they said together.

"Jinx!"

They broke into laughter, slapping high fives.

Games and Goodbyes

Wednesday flew by. Coach Dave worked on skills and drills. At two o'clock, Coach Dave announced, "Let's scrimmage!"

"Yay!" Tom cheered the loudest. He had been dying for a game.

"Dark jerseys against light jerseys," Coach Dave called out.

Tom skated over to Harty. "We're on the same team!"

"No cherry-picking!" warned Coach Dave. He dropped the puck. "Look for open ice!" He headed for the boards. "Show me your best!" And everyone did.

Thursday flew by. Coach Dave taught them six new plays and how to play safe. *Wow!* thought Tom. *He's a stickler for safety.*

"Keep your sticks down! Keep your heads up! Focus! Beware of the boards! An injured hockey player can't play hockey!" Coach Dave repeated his tips loud and clear. He banged the butt end of his stick when he saw something he liked. "Good work! Yes! Fantastic! Keep it clean." He turned his Flames cap around and scrubbed the ice with his stick as though he were cleaning it. "Scrub-a-dub-dub! No penalties here!" Everyone laughed.

The words stuck in Tom's brain. "Stick down. Head up. Focus." He managed to do things right even while his brain buzzed from all the thinking, listening, watching and remembering.

Before he knew it, it was two o'clock and

Coach Dave was announcing, "Enough! Let's scrimmage!"

"Yay!" the group cheered, circling around their coach.

"Sticks in!" he said. All the kids threw their sticks into the middle. Coach Dave divided them into two piles.

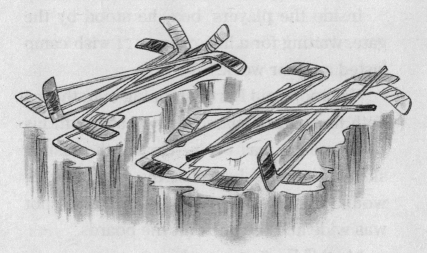

Tom and Harty grabbed theirs. They were on the same team. They raced to the bench and gulped back some water. They were ready to go.

On Friday afternoon when the scrimmage started, Tom felt like a pro. Every skill and trick was working for him. He could play and take instructions at the same time. And he was glad he was on the same team as Harty again.

Inside the players' box, he stood by the gate, waiting for a line change. "I wish camp lasted another week!"

"Me too," said Harty, stepping onto the ice with him. Harty snatched the puck with his stick and he was off — clearly the fastest skater at camp. Just past the blue line, he wound up and took a shot on net. The shot was wide and the puck hit the boards.

"Argh!" Harty groaned.

Tom kept quiet. He wished he knew what to say.

Harty hadn't scored a goal all week. His shots were always high or wide.

At three o'clock, when Champs Hockey Camp was nearly over, Coach Dave blew his whistle and signalled for everyone to meet at centre ice for a group photograph. The players dropped to one knee, their sticks balanced on the ice.

"Say 'Stanley Cup'!" Coach Dave snapped a few quick shots. Then he spoke seriously. "You're all fine team players and I am stressing the word 'team.' There is no 'I' in team. In hockey, you win as a team and you lose as a team. Good luck next season. And have fun! Play hockey because you want to!" He flipped his stick around and tapped the butt end twice.

While everyone was banging their stick on the ice, Harty got to his feet and skated over to the players' box. He picked up something from under the bench and returned to centre ice. Everyone was smiling except the coach. He just looked puzzled.

"Thank you, Coach Dave," said Harty, trying hard not to laugh, "from all of us." He presented the coach with a thank-you gift. It was a giant tape-ball, made from everyone's old sock tape.

"Wow! Thanks," said Coach Dave, with a chuckle. "You guys will always stay . . . er, I mean, *stick* . . . in my memory. Now, everyone on the blue line — with your right glove off."

What is Coach Dave up to now? wondered Tom, while he skated into place. When the line was complete, Coach Dave took off his own right glove and his Flames cap and skated down the line, looking each player right in the eye and shaking hand after hand. When he was done, all the players threw their gloves in the air. "Yay!" they cheered, circling around Coach Dave. "Woo hoo!"

"Now, go get your shorts on," said Coach Dave. "It's summer out there and the mosquitoes are hungry!"

When the players reached the dressing room, a surprise was waiting for them. Coach Dave had tucked a coupon into everyone's shoe: "GOOD FOR ONE FREE SLUSH DRINK."

— ● —

As Harty and Tom sat on the arena steps for the last time, watching cars pull into the parking lot, Tom got an idea. "How about sleeping over at my house tonight, if it's okay with our parents?"

"Sure!" Harty's face beamed. "I know my mom'll say yes — if she has time to drive me."

"There's my mom now!" Tom waited for her to park, and then he ran over to talk to her. She looked over at Harty and smiled.

Tom ran back to Harty, waving his arms. "You can come after dinner. And make sure you bring your hockey stick."

"My mom's here!" Harty's mom pulled into the lot and he ran to ask her.

"Yes!" he yelped, as she gave him the okay.

Their mothers got out of their cars for a chat.

"C'mon, Mom! Let's go!"

Once Harty's mom had directions to Tom's house, she looked at her watch. "Gee, I guess we should hustle. You guys live on the other side of town! Good thing I'm not working this weekend."

"See you soon!" said Harty.

"See you soon!" agreed Tom. He couldn't wait to show Harty his secret.

They drove off slurping their free slush drinks.

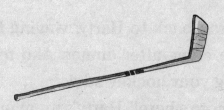

Practise
Practise
Practise

After dinner took forever to arrive. "Where is he?" Tom mumbled, peering down the street. He stickhandled a tennis ball up and down the driveway to pass the time.

Finally Harty's car drove up. Tom ran to greet him. They unloaded the car.

"See you tomorrow, around eleven," said Harty's mom. "Remember, you have a birthday party to go to at noon. Have fun tonight!" She waved goodbye.

"C'mon," said Tom. "Let's go." They raced to the backyard.

In Tom's backyard, giant truck tires leaned against a brick wall. An ice cream bucket filled with pucks sat on the sidewalk next to the house.

"It's target practice time!" smiled Tom, gearing into action. "This is the way I perfected my wicked slapshot." He grabbed a puck from the bucket, dropped it on the sidewalk and took a shot. "I've got some old crazy carpets, too, if you want to shoot from something slippery."

"This is awesome," said Harty. He put down his sleeping bag and reached for a puck. "I never practise at home."

"*Never?*" Tom couldn't imagine that.

"Never." Harty blushed.

The boys stood on the sidewalk, shooting puck after puck — aiming for the centres of the tires. They shot backhand and forehand. They practised all the shots Coach Dave taught them — flip shots, wrist shots, snap

shots. They stood on one foot, then two. They tried some wicked slapshots.

Harty followed Tom's lead, but he didn't score. The puck always hit the wall.

"I can't believe it," sighed Harty. "What am I doing wrong?"

"I don't know," said Tom. "You look good. And you've got good power. Let's just keep shooting."

Again, they shot puck after puck, this

time from the crazy carpets.

Bang! Thwack! Bang! Clunk!

Finally, Harty got close. "Yes! That one hit the side of the tire."

"Yahoo! Keep aiming for the centre, you'll get it!" cheered Tom. But, after another hour, Harty still didn't get one in the hole.

The screen door slammed and Tom's mom carried a tray of snacks to the picnic table: watermelon, veggies, crackers, pepperoni sticks and a pitcher of lemonade. "Your arms must be falling off!" she teased. "Here, recharge your batteries."

Harty put down his stick and rummaged through his overnight bag. "I brought some snacks, too." He pulled out a couple of chocolate bars and two cans of cola. He held up the pop. "Ever tried mixing this with lemonade? My friend Jake and I call it slug slime."

"Yuck!" said Tom's mom.

 "Yummm!" said Tom, mixing them each a glass. "Cheers, man."

"Cheers."

They clinked glasses. Tom swallowed a big mouthful. "Not bad," he admitted. They grabbed some pepperoni and went to collect the pucks scattered at the fence.

When they picked up their sticks again, Tom's mom had her digital camera and was taking pictures. "Now, smile, Tom. I know you're having fun."

"Mom, *pleeeeease!*" Tom made a face. She sure knew how to bug him.

Harty cracked up.

They kept shooting and she kept taking pictures.

When it got dark, Tom's dad pulled up in his truck.

"Hi, guys!"

"Hi Dad!" said Tom.

"Hey, how about some night lights? It's pitch-black out here!" He parked the truck on the cement pad so that the headlights shone on the targets. He switched the radio to Tom's station.

"Wow!" said Harty, looking impressed. "Now this is the coolest place in town!"

"You must be Harty," said Tom's dad. "I've been hearing about hockey camp all week." He grabbed his stick from the garage and took a few shots. "Oops. That tire's a good goalie," he laughed. He dropped the last puck and took another shot. It went right into the hole.

"Now let's see *your* stuff," said Tom's dad, glancing at Harty.

Harty looked down, embarrassed. "I'm hopeless," he said.

"What?" said Tom's dad, shaking his head. "Tom says you're the fastest thing on skates."

"My shots are hopeless."

Tom's dad helped him with his grip and set-up. Still, Harty did not score.

———•———

Totally exhausted, the boys spread out their sleeping bags in the back of the truck.

Just before closing their eyes, Tom said, "I knew the best thing about summer would be hockey camp."

"No kidding," said Harty. "It was a blast. I wish we were pros and Coach Dave was our coach."

"He rocks!" said Tom.

Within minutes, they fell asleep with their NHL dreams.

E-mail

Breakfast came too soon. Tom's mom made whole wheat pancakes with fresh strawberries and sausage patties.

She poured some juice and turned to the computer. "Look, you guys. You've already got an e-mail from Coach Dave!"

There on the screen was a photo of them all at centre ice — with a caption: Champs Hockey Champions.

"I got it, too!" said Harty, seeing his e-mail address in the list.

"You look like a bunch of wet-heads,"

joked Tom's mom. "Hey, hope you two had showers last night!"

Their faces turned bright red.

Tom's mom rolled her eyes.

"We're busted," said Tom, piling up pancakes.

After they had stuffed themselves, Tom said "Harty, let's play one-on-one street hockey till you get picked up."

They had barely started when Harty's mom pulled into the driveway. She was in a hurry. "Hi guys. Gotta go, Harty. I have to get you to this party on time. It's a movie, remember — and it's a long way back." She popped the trunk. "How was last night?"

"We practised shooting pucks," answered Harty, loading his stuff in.

"Really?" said his mom, smiling. "A whole week wasn't enough, eh?"

"Nope! We kept going till really late." Harty hesitated for a second. "Hey, Mom —

does Grampa still have those old tires?"

"I think so." His mom looked puzzled. "What for?"

"Thanks a ton," Harty shouted, waving wildly as they drove away. "Bye!"

"Bye!" Tom waved back, until the car disappeared around the corner.

———— ● ————

Later that day, Tom flipped through the photos on his mom's digital camera. Suddenly,

something stood out in every shot of Harty. "That's it!" he cried. He hurried to the computer and found Harty's e-mail address from Coach Dave's message. He began to type.

```
Hi Harty,

Keep your eyes open when you
shoot. And don't take them off
the target. That should do the
trick. Maybe a hat trick! Take
a good look at the photos I'm
attaching. Have fun playing
hockey this winter.

Your friend, Tom
```

The phone rang. It was Mark. He was home from his trip and looking for a street hockey game.

Tom called Jordan. Jordan was ready to practise what he learned at goalie camp.

The doorbell rang. Stuart's ankle was better and his three cousins were in town. They all loved hockey.

Tom grabbed his stick and a tennis ball.

As they set up the nets, Tom announced, "I'm going to make you guys drink slug slime after our first period."

"What?" they screeched.

"You'll love it."

While Tom played street hockey with his friends, an e-mail arrived in his inbox.

`Hi Tom,`

`Thanks for the tip. I'm going to try really hard to keep my eyes open and on the target. My Grampa is setting up some tires tonight. And I'm going to practise every day I can.`

`Your friend, Harty`

`P.S. Rent the movie Wartman on Ice. It rocks!`

The Tournament

Five months went by. By the middle of January Tom's hockey team, the Glenlake Hawks, was having its best season ever. Tom loved playing centre with Mark on right wing, Stuart on defence and Jordan in goal. He loved playing anytime, anywhere — on the street, at the arenas and on the outdoor rinks.

———— ● ————

It was the first day of the big city tournament. Tom sat in the back seat of his dad's truck as it made its way over the snow-covered roads to Centennial Arena, lost in his own thoughts.

He took a deep breath. The closer they got to the arena, the tighter his stomach knotted. *Okay, focus*, he told himself. In his mind he could see the puck behind the net. He could see himself reach out and make the perfect wraparound shot. *Yep.* The puck whipped into the net, right past the goalie's glove.

"There's Stuart's van," said Tom's mom, interrupting his concentration. The parking lot was packed. "And . . . oh good . . . Coach Howie's car."

Tom smiled. It always felt good recognizing some cars, because it meant he was at the right arena at the right time and his friends were, too.

Tom's dad carried the bag while Tom stickhandled an invisible puck along the sidewalk and through the arena doors.

Dozens of people swarmed the entrance

area. Many were bundled in bulky jackets, holding blankets and drinking hot chocolate.

Tom scanned the message board, looking for his dressing room number. He grabbed his bag and headed down the hall. Some of the kids he passed were wearing team colours he'd never seen before. Then Mark brushed by him with a slap on the back.

"Hey, Tom, I'm ready for them."

"Me too," said Jordan, a few steps behind, pulling his huge goalie bag.

"Me too," agreed Tom.

The team suited up.

Coach Howie stood in the middle of the dressing room with the league stats from the local paper. "Hawks, we are undefeated! And Jordan holds the city's shutout record!" he announced.

Everyone cheered.

"Hawks, we are rated Number One!" bellowed Coach Howie.

Everyone started chanting, "We're Number One. We're Number One."

Tom knew they were good, but he didn't know they were this good.

"Now, let's play hockey!" shouted Coach Howie.

Hawks vs. Bulldogs

Tom's heart raced as the team filed out of the dressing room. He looked up when they reached the ice. The stands were full. He could see his grandma and grandpa. They waved.

The gates opened and the players stepped onto the ice. They skated in circles and warmed up with quick starts and stops. The clock counted down. At the whistle, the team gathered around their goalie and cheered loud and strong, "HAWKS! HAWKS! HAWKS!" Tom's line took their places on the ice while the rest of the players headed for the box.

Tom set up at centre. He looked quickly at the opposing player. His Northland Bulldogs jersey was tucked into the right side of his pants. This was exactly how Tom wore his own jersey, which was exactly how Wayne Gretzky had worn his. Tom looked at the player's face. He could see some red hair poking out of the helmet. "Harty?" he asked. A smile spread across his face. "Is that you?"

"Tom?" replied Harty. His smile was wider.

The ref dropped the puck. Tom took the faceoff and raced down the ice. He passed the puck to Mark. Mark passed it back to Tom. A Bulldog blocked him. Harty grabbed the puck and shot it along the boards. Tom and Harty raced for the puck, only to be stopped by the whistle the instant Harty touched it.

"Number fifteen Northland — two minutes for tripping," shouted the ref.

A Bulldog headed for the penalty box as both coaches waved their players off the ice. The lines changed.

Tom gulped back some water, watching the game and waiting for his next shift. The puck crisscrossed the ice end to end, again and again.

C'mon, Hawks! Tom willed a power play goal. *C'mon! C'mon! There are only four Bulldogs out there!*

Mark dug the puck out of the corner. He passed it to Stuart. Stuart took a shot, aiming for the five-hole. The Bulldogs' goalie blocked it, rebounding the puck to Mark. Mark took a shot. Tom looked at the clock. Two minutes were up. A new Bulldog launched onto the ice.

Coach Howie smiled. "This is a great game. These Bulldogs are good. We can't let up. It's going to take everything we have to win this tournament."

Tom moved along the bench. He kept his eyes on #66 of the Bulldogs.

"Go Hawks, go!" Tom cheered with his team, banging his stick on the boards.

Breakaway

Near the end of the third period, the score was still 0–0.

A Bulldog iced the puck. The whistle blew. The lines changed.

Tom set up at the faceoff, facing Harty. Their eyes focused on the ice as the linesman dropped the puck. Tom won the faceoff and dropped it back to Stuart. Stuart handled the puck as though it were glued to his stick. A Bulldog player was bearing down on him so he passed the puck over to Mark. The pass was perfect, but a Bulldog winger stole the puck and passed it to Harty.

Suddenly Harty had a breakaway! He

roared down the ice, his head up and his eyes on Jordan. Mark and Tom chased after him, but Harty had the jump on them. He wound up and let it fly with a wicked slapshot. The puck whizzed through the air, hitting the back of the net "top shelf" — where Momma hides the cookies.

The ref's whistle blew as he signalled.

"Goal!"

The Bulldog bench screamed and the crowd went crazy.

Tom looked at Harty, who was bending over to catch his breath. For a split second, he saw the number 66 upside-down on the back of his jersey. It looked like . . . 99!

Tom felt bad for Jordan. His shutout record was blown. He felt bad for their defence. And with three seconds left in the game, he felt bad for his team, about to lose and be no longer "undefeated." But Tom felt good about something.

He and Harty set up for the last faceoff. As the ref held up the puck between them, Tom flipped his stick around and tapped the butt end twice.

The teams and the spectators looked puzzled.

Harty smiled at Tom. "Thanks."

The puck dropped. The clock counted down 3 . . . 2 . . . 1 . . . *Buzzzzzzzz*. The Bulldogs cir-

cled around Harty, cheering and celebrating.

As the Zamboni's engine revved, the teams skated into lines and shook hands.

When Tom and Harty met, they both flipped their sticks around and tapped the butt ends twice.

Tom's team filed back to their dressing room and slumped on the benches, still in shock.

"What was *that*?" asked Jordan.

"One wicked slapshot," said Tom. "One wicked slapshot!"

"I didn't even see it coming," sighed Jordan.

Hockey
Forever

The arena steps were covered with fresh snow and the parking lot had ice thick enough to skate on. White clouds billowed from the cars as they warmed up. Tom and Harty stood side by side, downing slush drinks.

"See you tomorrow," said Harty. "Maybe both our teams will get to the finals."

"See you tomorrow," said Tom. "Now *you've* got a wicked slapshot!"

"Thanks!" Harty beamed. "Your pictures sure helped. I keep my eyes open now. And, boy, did I practise!"

A van pulled up with Tom's three friends in the back. Stuart called out, "Hey guys, shinny game at Chinook Park at two! See you there!"

"Want to play?" Tom asked Harty.

"Sure, I'll play 99 times a day!" he answered, tapping the butt end of his stick twice. And they both cracked up.